APOLLO
IN COLORLAND

By CC Rechsteiner &
Illustrated by Patrick Williams

Apollo in Colorland
2014 by CC Rechsteiner
First Edition

Published by:
Gelinda Rechsteiner

Distributed by:
www.ccrechsteiner.com

Illustrated by: Patrick Williams
www.pwilliamsart.com

Edited by
Celeste Lauro

Library of Congress Control Number: 2014913035

Throughout this beautifully illustrated story, Apollo teaches your child, through jungle animals, the concept of rejection, acceptance, and how everyone is the same though they look different. Apollo (the turtle) lands on Colorland where all the animals have bright colors. However, unlike the bright colored animals, Apollo's colors are "dull and green." Once the other animals see this, they do not want anything to do with him. Rex (the king) teaches the bright colored animals that even though Apollo looks different he is still an animal just like them.

PRINTED IN SOUTH KOREA BY:
Star Print Brokers, Inc.
Bellevue, Washington
StarPrintBrokers.com

ISBN: 978-0-578-14578-5

DEDICATED TO:

Mom for helping me bring my dream into a reality,
and dad for supporting me every step of the way.

Mary Carbone and Sharon Brucato for helping me throughout
this process, out of the kindness of their hearts.

John Christl for challenging me for 16 years.

In Memory of Jordan

In a Kingdom called Colorland there lives many
animals that are very bright in color...

...like a bright pink elephant, a bright orange parrot, a bright purple monkey, and a bright blue giraffe!

Miss Bubbles is a pink elephant that is very sweet, kind, and always smiling. Mister Squawky is a bossy orange parrot!

Rascal is a mischievous purple monkey, and Lilly is a shy and timid blue giraffe.

The King of Colorland is a bright yellow lion named Rex.

He has a family and is very kind to all the animals in his Kingdom.

The King shows his kindness by letting his

animals play games like Hide-and-Go-Seek . . .

They also play Red-light / Green-light!

The elephant, parrot, monkey, and giraffe enjoy everything they do in Colorland . . .

even learning how to read and write, and do math in school.

But, what made the elephant, parrot, monkey and giraffe

the happiest was their colors!

One day, a friendly turtle by the name of Apollo was taking a relaxing boat ride when all of a sudden a great storm blew him far across the sea to the Kingdom of Colorland!

When the brightly colored animals heard there was a new animal in their Kingdom, they were all very excited. "There is a visitor in our land!" screeched Mister Squawky.

"What does he look like and where did he come from?" cried the other animals.

"Maybe he will be pink like me," smiled Miss Bubbles.

"Or maybe he will be blue and tall like me," whispered Lilly.

Swinging from the tree onto Miss Bubbles' back,

Rascal cried out, "Hurry, hurry! Let's go see the visitor!"

Lilly and Miss Bubbles, with Rascal on her back, followed Mister Squawky with great excitement down the path to see the visitor.

When the animals came upon the visitor,

they noticed Mister Squawky was staring at him.

"It's a turtle! And he is not colorful like us at all!" cried Mister Squawky!

"...or tall and blue like me!" whispered Lilly, timidly.

"What is wrong with him? He is dull and green! Dull and green!" cried Rascal!

The friendly little turtle walked over to the animals with a big smile and said
"Hi, my name is Apollo, and I come from a land very far away. May I visit your land?"

"I should say not," squawked Mister Squawky.

"Why not?" asked Apollo sadly. "Because you have a dull and green color,
dull and green color!" jabbered Rascal, swinging in a tree.

"My colors may be different, but can't we be friends?"

asked Apollo. "No!" screeched Mister Squawky.

"Go home!" stomped Miss Bubbles. "Go now! Go now!" cried Rascal.

Lilly, agreeing with her friends, whispered, "leave!"

When King Rex learned how his animals treated the turtle, he went to them and roared with anger. "I will punish you for not treating the turtle with kindness!" "But he is not like us," cried Mister Squawky. "He is not big and pink like me," said Miss Bubbles.

"Or tall and blue like me," whispered Lilly. "Come and see, come and see!

He is a dull and green color, dull and green," chattered Rascal. "So what?" roared Rex!

"He is still an animal like you. The only difference is his color!"

King Rex decided to punish the animals and turned their bright colors into the same dull and green color as the turtle's. At first, they were very upset and cried for a long time over losing their bright colors.

The parrot, monkey, elephant, and giraffe then understood

when they saw themselves that the King was right.

They were still the same animals as before - just with a different color.

"I am sorry," squawked Mister Squawky. "Me too, me too," jabbered Rascal.

"Come play with us," smiled Miss Bubbles. "Please," whispered Lilly, "let's be friends".

Once again, the elephant, parrot, monkey, and giraffe were happy

because they were having fun with their new friend playing Hide-and-Go-Seek...

and Red-light/Green-light.

They even let Apollo learn to read and write and do math with them in school!

When King Rex saw his animals letting the turtle join them, he was very pleased.

So he changed their colors into what you see today ... a gray elephant ... a green parrot

... a brown monkey ... and a yellow giraffe! And Apollo stayed just the way he was!